W9-AYD-135

Fat Fanny,
Beanpole Bertha,
AND THE BOYS

 A Richard Jackson Book

Also by Barbara Ann Porte

RUTHANN AND HER PIG

Fat Fanny,
Beanpole Bertha,
AND THE BOYS

by BARBARA ANN PORTE

illustrated by MAXIE CHAMBLISS

ORCHARD BOOKS   NEW YORK

Orchard Books, 95 Madison Avenue, New York, New York 10016

Manufactured in the United States of America.
Book design by Mina Greenstein.
The text of this book is set in 12 point Fairfield Medium.
The illustrations are pencil drawings reproduced in halftone.
10   9   8   7   6   5   4   3

Library of Congress Cataloging-in-Publication Data
Porte, Barbara Ann.
Fat Fanny, Beanpole Bertha, and the boys / by Barbara Ann Porte ;
illustrated by Maxie Chambliss.   p.   cm.
Summary: When Bertha's father vanishes in the Bermuda Triangle,
and Fanny's theater agent parents are secretly divorced,
the girls decide to teach Fanny's triplet brothers to tap-dance to
raise money.
"A Richard Jackson book."
ISBN 0-531-05928-6.   ISBN 0-531-08528-7 (lib.)
[1. Mystery and detective stories.]   I. Chambliss, Maxie, ill.
II. Title.   PZ7.P7995Fat   1991   [Fic]—dc20   90-7686

To KIRSTAN and DOUGLAS, with love

CONTENTS

Fat Fanny,
Beanpole Bertha,
AND THE BOYS

Fanny and Bertha

"FAT FANNY got an A, and Beanpole Bertha got another," read the note that Stewie Hochman tried to pass to Billy Botwin the day their math tests were returned. Cynthia Reilly intercepted the note and put it into her pocket. She read it aloud in the school yard at recess.

"I could choke that Stewie Hochman," Fanny said. Bertha, though, was unperturbed.

"What's a D student know, anyhow?" she asked.

Stewie Hochman's family has moved away, but the names Fat Fanny and Beanpole Bertha have lingered. Not that the girls care *that* much. They have far more pressing matters on their minds. It's a stroke of luck for them having each other. They've been best friends since kindergarten.

"Go stand by that sign," a teacher in the school yard told Fanny, pointing, the very first day of school. So that's what Fanny did. She stood and waited patiently, alone on line. Her mother had dropped her off early on the way to the airport. She'd offered to stay, but Fanny said no. She didn't want the other children to think she was a baby. Fanny was all dressed up in new clothes: a white middy blouse, a navy skirt, matching tights, and lace-up shoes. Her hair hung down her back in one long and very thick braid, tied at the end with red ribbon. It wasn't quite blond and it wasn't quite brown. Fanny was a bit plump even then, but certainly not fat.

"Just look at that face!" grown-ups sometimes said, pinching Fanny's cheeks, meaning she was pretty.

That minute, though, Fanny was trying only not to look anxious. She examined the ground, then heard a voice say, "Hello there, little girl. What's your name? This is my girl. Her name is Bertha. Please, will you be her friend?"

Fanny looked up. A tall woman in a flowered blouse and a long red skirt was smiling down at her. Fanny thought she'd never seen such a friendly face. The woman was resting her hands on the metal bar of a baby stroller. It was divided into three compartments. In each one sat a bald-headed baby, barefoot and kicking, in yellow pajamas. On one baby's head was perched his green beret. The other two were waving theirs. The babies all looked exactly alike. Running circles around them was a girl Fanny's age, apparently Bertha.

She looked a bit like a Gypsy to Fanny, with a wiry build and dark curly hair. Her chin was pointed and she had very bright, very brown eyes. She wore a red checkered dress and a tiny silver ring in each earlobe. She had exactly the sort of looks Fanny admired, plus her family seemed so interesting. Why wouldn't Fanny want to be Bertha's friend?

"What's your name?" the stroller woman asked again.

"Fanny," said Fanny. "I'm Fanny Barton."

"That's a nice name," said the woman. She leaned down and kissed Bertha good-bye, then walked away, pushing the stroller. "You girls look after each other now," she called back over her shoulder, as she left the school yard. From that day to this the girls have tried, though the past two years have been hard. They've had major dislocations in their lives beside which names like "Fat" and "Beanpole" seem almost like nothing.

Bertha and Her Family

THIS IS BERTHA'S FAMILY: Bertha herself, nearly eleven now and in fifth grade; her mother, Ms. Berenice Segal; and Bertha's three brothers, Marvin, Matthew, and Marcus, called Marc for short except by his mother, who doesn't care for nicknames. They have a father, too, but he is lost, officially a missing person for the past two years, ever since his plane strayed from its course and disappeared over the Bermuda Triangle. He was on a business trip—a traveling salesman selling military hardware.

"Lost is lost," Ms. Segal says. "It doesn't mean he's never coming back. He's only been delayed." But this delay has complications. Bertha's mother cannot collect on her husband's life-insurance policy, for instance. She goes to work instead, putting Bertha in charge of the triplets whenever necessary.

"Thank goodness for Bertha," she frequently says. "I don't know how we'd manage without her." Bertha, of course, is pleased to hear this. It's nice to be appreciated. But even so, keeping up with the boys is a lot of hard work.

"It's running me ragged," she sometimes tells Fanny. She worries she's not up to the job. When she thinks of all she needs to do, she feels tiny fingers clutching at her stomach. She confides in Fanny: "I think I'm getting an ulcer."

"You have to eat more," Fanny advises. Her father once had one. "Try chocolate milk, ice cream, frozen custard, hot fudge sauce."

"I don't have time," says Bertha. That's the truth, plus so much extra work has taken the edge off her appetite.

"It's a good thing it's only temporary," Bertha's mother says. "Just until your father gets back." Ms. Segal also works hard. She has two regular jobs in addition to mother. She'd probably be rail-thin herself by now, but both her jobs are in restaurants.

She works at Hallie's Hotcake House from six A.M. to two P.M. She wears a red uniform, a white apron, and a white chef's hat with red letters on its brim that spell "Hallie's Hotcake Helper." She stands behind a hot griddle in the middle of the store, flipping hotcakes. Customers call out suggestions. "Make mine brown around the edges." "I hate my hotcakes over-cooked."

"Right," says Bertha's mother, smiling. Smiling is part of her job, but she would probably smile anyway. She has a sunny disposition. Also, she's good at what she does. She made hot-cakes as a child at home in Iowa.

Her second job is chef at Caesar's Pizza Palace from eight P.M. until midnight. She wears a white apron over her everyday clothes and a white chef's hat that says "Caesar's" in black script letters. She stands in the window of the store pounding pie dough, then tossing the circles into the air. Next, she adds the main ingredients, sauce, cheese, and olive oil, and last of all the extras, sausage, pepperoni, salami, anchovies, olives. Then she puts the pies into the oven to bake them. Customers offer suggestions here also. "Lots of cheese." "More pepperoni, please."

"Right," Bertha's mother says, smiling. She's very good at this job, too. Well, she's good at it now. When she first saw the sign in the window that read, "Night chef needed, apply within," she didn't know anything about pizza except how to eat it, but she knew she needed the job. "Apple, spinach, sweet-potato, squash; pie is pie," she told herself, and went inside and applied. "Of course I can," she told Caesar. Then she sent Bertha to the library to borrow some books on Italian cuisine. She studied them carefully.

Between jobs, Bertha's mother goes home, naps when she has enough time, showers, straightens the house, fixes meals, washes clothes, opens mail, pays bills, and reads to the children. You'd think she might get discouraged even with Bertha's help, but she doesn't. Ms. Segal is an optimist by nature. However bleak life seems, she's positive it will get better and, in this case, why not? Wouldn't almost anything seem an improvement?

Perhaps, but Bertha's always been a worrier. However bad things are, she worries they'll get worse. Her mother could lose a job for instance. She could lose them both. Where would that leave the family? Bertha isn't sure what else her mother knows how to do besides cook, at least in Tenafly, New Jersey, the town where they live. If they were living in the country, now, it would be a different story.

Bertha's mother knows how to farm. It's what her family did for a living in Iowa when she was growing up. She understands grazing cows, growing crops, raising flocks. She can call pigs and slop them. "Here, suey, suey, suey," she sometimes trills, just to show Bertha how. Once she won a contest, but that was long ago. In Tenafly there is no call for it. There are no farms. There are no pigs.

"Maybe we should move to Iowa," Bertha suggests every now and then. She dreams of life in the country, secure and content. But moving costs money. Even just renting a van is expensive.

"Besides, how would your father find us when he gets back?" her mother asked the last time Bertha suggested moving.

Bertha saw her mother's point. "Right," she said, and frowned.

"You're going to get wrinkles," Bertha's mother warned her.

She seems to be getting them now. See her standing in the

kitchen, wrinkling her forehead, making all those furrows, frowning at her brothers and at Fanny. She wishes they would hurry. Fanny has stopped by on her way to school, as she often does, to eat her second breakfast with them. Fanny thinks breakfasts at Bertha's house are much better than at hers. This morning it's pizza—leftover, reheated pizza Bertha's mother brought home from Caesar's last night. Leftovers are an extra. They go with her job. Fanny loves pizza.

"It's got several of your basic food groups in it," she points out.

"Eat faster," Bertha says, spreading peanut butter on a narrow edge of pizza crust. "We're going to be late." She has given the center parts with sausage and cheese to the others. Bertha doesn't care for pizza, but she loves peanut butter.

"Yuck," say the triplets, making faces at her meal.

"Astronauts eat peanut butter," Bertha tells them. "It's high-energy food, full of protein." Actually, Bertha has no idea what astronauts eat, but it sounds good to her. If she were an astronaut, peanut butter is what she'd pick to take on her trips. It's so convenient and easy to fix. In fact, it's what she packs almost every day for lunch, for all of them.

Finally, everyone is finished eating. Bertha locks the door behind them and tucks the key on its string inside her blouse, and they walk down the street together. They wave at the neighbors watching out their windows. The neighbors keep their eyes on the children. Morning and night, they check on them to be sure they're all right. It's reassuring to Bertha knowing she has grown-ups to turn to in a pinch.

"Thank goodness for good neighbors," Bertha's mother often says. "I don't know what we'd do without them."

"Isn't that what neighbors are for?" they say when she thanks them. "Besides," they add, "it's only temporary." Bertha's mother is pleased to hear them say this. It confirms her own opinion about her husband's coming back. Bertha, on the other hand, worries what they mean by it. Perhaps they only mean it's temporary until the fatherless family gets back on its feet.

Well, they're all on their feet this minute. Bertha's mother is standing on hers flipping hotcakes at Hallie's, and the children are walking to school. "Walk faster," says Bertha. "You're going to be late."

Bertha loves school and looks forward to going. It's a chance to sit down, lean back in her chair, put her feet up on the desk rungs. She likes knowing someone else is in charge.

"ELBOWS OFF THE TABLE, please. Sit up straight," Ms. Maxwell, her teacher, tells her, but she smiles as she says it. Ms. Maxwell likes Bertha, and also worries about her. She thinks she's much too thin, and tired looking. "She's only ten, but she looks as if she needs a vacation," Ms. Maxwell sometimes tells her husband.

Even so, Bertha is one of her best students. Gym is the only subject Bertha doesn't care for. "If I wanted to be on my feet running, I could stay home," she sometimes tells Fanny. But what she really hates is the gym suit, blue bloomers with elasticized legs that hang, too loose, on her own. "It's true. I look like a beanpole," she says. Then she thinks of poor Fanny, and imagines how she feels about the way she looks in hers.

"I feel ill," Fanny sometimes says, hoping to get out of gym. But it's required. Fanny often eats a little snack before or after, hoping it will make her feel better. "Plus I can use the energy," she says.

The triplets don't have gym. They're only in third grade. You have to be in fourth for gym. They just have recess. That is the reason Bertha exercises them after school. "If you don't stretch, you won't grow," she tells them. When she was their age, she was quite a bit taller than they are. She also took gymnastics. Their father wasn't lost yet, and there was money for lessons. Now, of course, they're out of the question. But Bertha sees no reason not to teach her brothers what she knows.

"Bend, stretch, squat, leap. Warm-ups are important," Bertha chants after school, as she demonstrates how. She has dragged an old mattress from the garage onto the lawn for the lesson.

"Ummm," say the triplets, observing. They'd rather be running around on their own, but go along with her plan because it's better than homework, which Bertha also supervises. Fanny is sitting on the grass, watching, and chewing thoughtfully on a cold hotcake from Hallie's. Where does Bertha get so much energy? Fanny wonders.

"I think you're wasting your time," she says in a while.

"I beg your pardon?" says Bertha, who at that precise minute is standing on her head. It's hard for her to hear with all that blood rushing back and forth between her ears. Also, Fanny has spoken with a last bit of hotcake still in her mouth. Bertha rights herself, then sits beside her friend. Fanny swallows.

"I said," she repeats, "you're all wasting your time in Tenafly. What the boys ought to do is learn tap. As cute as they are, and so small, if they knew how to tap dance they could do it on television. They'd be famous. And get rich. You'd all get rich and famous." Fanny knows about such things from her parents. Both of them are talent scouts. They have an agency.

"Television?" says Bertha, sounding doubtful. Immediately she starts to think of obstacles likely to block their path to stardom. The boys are only seven in the first place. Bertha thinks seven is too young to hold down a job. There is their mother, in the second place, who takes a dim view of television. And finally, as Bertha points out to Fanny, "Dancing lessons cost money."

"Where there's a will there's a way," says Fanny, unfazed. "People's fortunes change every day. Why shouldn't yours?" Bertha's fortune has already changed, of course. Her father has disappeared. What Fanny has in mind is a turn for the better. "Your problem is you never look on the bright side," she says to Bertha.

It's not the first time Bertha's heard that. Is Fanny right? Could life be about to improve in the Segal household?

Fanny and Her Family

THIS IS FANNY'S FAMILY: Fanny herself, and her parents, Muffin and Bernie. They don't care to be called Mom and Dad. "It doesn't sound professional," they tell Fanny. They try to think chic. "Muffin and Bernie, Inc., Fresh Faces a Specialty" is the name of their agency.

Also living in the house is Fanny's nanny, Hildegarde Humbolt, who is six foot two with no shoes, and from Texas. "Big Hildy" most people called her before she moved East. "Fanny can call me Nanny," she announced the day she arrived. "It's easy to say and it's got a nice ring."

Fanny's parents were a bit surprised. They had practiced saying "governess" for weeks. Still, they hadn't been talent agents all that time for nothing. They talked it over. "It certainly is catchy," they told each other, pleased. When Fanny finally began to speak, the very first word she said was "Nanny." She said it happily for years.

Eventually, though, as she matured, Fanny came to believe having a nanny was babyish. No doubt she was right. But by then Hildegarde had been with them so long she was almost like family. What would she do if she left them? Where would she go? And how would they manage without her? Fanny may have been too old to have a nanny, but she was still far too young to be left all alone when her parents were gone overnight.

"You just call me Hildegarde, then, from now on," Nanny told her. Ever since, that's what Fanny's called her.

And what of Fanny's parents? Where are they gone to so much of the time? Traveling is in the nature of their business. They traipse back and forth from coast to coast, New York to California, California to New York. That's where deals are made. Deals are how they earn their living. It's a good living, but a bit hard on the family.

"New Jersey's a coast, too," Fanny used to complain to Hildegarde. Hildegarde was sympathetic, but only to a point.

"Believe me, there are worse things in life than having rich parents who travel," she said. "It certainly beats dipping sheep in the sun." Hildegarde had grown up on a sheep ranch and worked summers beside her parents, who were ranch hands. She had in mind the sheep they used to run through vats of chemicals every August to detick them. "Trust me," she told

Fanny. "Your life could be much worse." Fanny, who was barely nine at the time, trusted Hildegarde. She was also about to find out for herself how right Hildegarde was.

"FANNY, DEAR. Come here," her mother called to her one Sunday morning nearly two years ago. "Bernie and I have something to tell you." Fanny joined her parents in the study. She sat beside her mother at one end of the long brown leather sofa. Her father sat cater-cornered from them in a high-backed wooden chair. His legs were crossed and he had a newspaper on his lap, opened to the theater section. Fanny carelessly stuck a strand of her hair into her mouth, chewed on it, and waited hopefully. Perhaps, she thought, her parents were going to Europe soon on business and planning to take her along. She'd been once before, but she hadn't been old enough at the time to remember most of what she saw. On the other hand, maybe all of them were only going out for dinner later that day, and Fanny was about to be told to put on her new pink guimpe and navy pinafore.

"Pay attention, Fanny. This is important," Fanny's father said. "Your mother and I have gotten a divorce."

"Gotten?" Fanny said, stunned. Perhaps she'd heard wrong. Maybe her father really had said, "Your mother and I are getting a divorce." Then there still would be time. But time to do what?

Muffin was speaking. Fanny tried to pay attention. It wasn't easy. A low-grade buzzing in her head kept getting in the way.

She did hear her mother say, "The main thing is you're not to worry. The divorce is between your father and me. It hasn't anything to do with you. You'll see. Your life will go on the same as before."

"Right," said Bernie. "The important thing is your mother and I still love you. That hasn't changed, and it never will."

"Right," said Muffin. "It's not your divorce and it isn't your fault."

Well, of course it wasn't Fanny's fault. No one had even asked her opinion. "Why?" Fanny asked her parents now.

Her parents looked at each other. Her mother said, "I know it's difficult for a child to understand. Your father and I still care deeply about each other, but we find we've grown apart."

"See," Bernie said, "except for the business and you, we don't seem to have much in common anymore."

Fanny stared in disbelief. Herself and the business. It seemed quite a lot to Fanny. She didn't point it out, though. She was, for the moment, speechless. It was taking all her concentration to keep from throwing up. If she had been standing, she would have had to sit. Her parents went on speaking in cheerful tones, in tandem. It was as though having gotten over the main part of their message, they found the rest easy. Fanny shook her head, as if to clear it. That was when she heard one of them say, "You needn't tell anyone either. We've decided, for the time being, to keep it private."

"I beg your pardon," said Fanny, shocked into finding her voice.

"It's nobody's business, really," said her mother.

"It wouldn't be good for our image," said her father. "Movie stars get divorced, not their agents."

"What your father means is people see us as a team," Muffin added. "We've always been a partnership. It could be bad for business." Well, Fanny had always seen them as a team, too. But they didn't seem to think about that. "Also, there are your grandparents to consider," Muffin said, meaning her own parents, who live in Vermont. Bernie's parents had passed away when Fanny still was an infant. "A divorce in the family would kill them."

Bernie nodded in agreement.

They were exaggerating of course. No one really dies just from hearing bad news. What Muffin meant was her parents would disapprove.

"Mum's the word, then," said Bernie. He chucked Fanny on the chin.

"We'll just keep it under our hats," Muffin said. She pinched Fanny's nearest cheek. Fine for her to say. She has so many hats, thought Fanny. What about me?

"Don't you think someone is bound to notice when one of you moves out?" Fanny was not yet willing to ask which one.

"Ah," said Bernie. "That's the good part."

"We've worked it out," said Muffin. "No one's moving anyplace. Both of us are staying here, the same as always."

Bernie explained the plan to Fanny. "We're going to coordinate our business trips. When your mother is home, I'll be away."

"And when your father is here, I'll be someplace else," Muffin said. "It won't be any problem at all pretending we're still married. Of course you'll stay put the same as now. When both of us are gone, you'll still have Hildegarde to watch you."

An easy enough plan, perhaps, for Fanny's parents. They're in show business. Pretending is part of their job. They've had practice. But Fanny isn't in show business. She isn't even in junior high. Her parents might as well have said, "Fanny, darling, don't talk anymore." Didn't they remember their childhoods at all? Fanny, of course, knew the truth. Every time she opened her mouth from then on, she'd be in danger of giving the secret away. Except, possibly, when she was eating. It's hard to talk with a mouth full of food. It's also hard to feel sad when you're eating something truly delicious.

FANNY KNOWS THIS from experience. For nearly two years now she's kept her parents' secret, but she's gained a lot of weight. See her at the kitchen table, a fifth grader, eating her after-school snack: lemon pudding cupcakes with icing, a chocolate malted milk, and a caramel apple on a stick.

"I'm glad to see you're eating fruit," Hildegarde says, watching. She does not approve of Fanny's diet. "It isn't natural," she says. She herself eats health foods—bean curd, lentil stew, yogurt—and bakes oat-bran raisin muffins that she serves with

22

herbal teas. "It's what keeps me so healthy," she tells anyone who will listen. She may be correct. Or, on the other hand, it may be mostly a matter of genes. One thing is certain: Hildegarde has wonderful teeth, while Fanny required a half-dozen fillings just in the past year. "It's all that sugar you eat," Hildegarde tells her.

Hildegarde would put her foot down, except she lacks authority in this area. Fanny gets an allowance to spend as she likes. "To teach her the value of money," Muffin and Bernie explain, almost weekly. Fanny spends it mostly on snacks. Hildegarde thinks if Fanny had to pay for her fillings, *that* might

teach her the value of money. But she doesn't say so to the Bartons. Instead, she tells her brother Henry, on the telephone. He still lives in Texas, where he runs a filling station, car wash, and repair shop.

"It hurts my heart," she tells him, "to see the child in this state." Naturally, she doesn't mean New Jersey. She means so anxious all the time and out of shape.

"She probably just needs a hobby to take her mind off herself," says Henry.

Hildegarde raises the subject with Fanny. "I think a girl your age should have an outside interest. Maybe you'd like to take some sort of lessons after school," she suggests.

The idea of lessons isn't new. Fanny's parents are talent agents after all. They've always had high hopes for her. They named her Fanny after Fanny Brice, the stage and movie star who played Baby Snooks on radio for years. "Snookums" Fanny's father even called her for a time.

Fanny looks at Hildegarde now and considers lessons; there was ballet at five, piano at six, then, briefly, the accordion, and for several months there was a cello in her life. She'd taken elocution at eight and emoting at nine. It's hard to imagine what's left.

"What sort of lessons do you have in mind?" she asks.

"Whatever you like. It's up to you," says Hildegarde. "If it were me, though, I'd take the saxophone."

"Saxophone?" Fanny tries to picture Hildegarde playing.

She sees her, tall and slim, her dark eyes narrowed, her long hair flowing, lips puckered, cheeks puffed out . . . blowing.

"Sure," says Hildegarde. "When I was a child in Texas, there was a cowboy who played one every Saturday on the radio. He could play anything. He blew high notes and low notes, fast notes and slow notes. At the end of each show he made his saxophone talk. Sometimes it told a story. Let me tell you, there is nothing more adorable than a saxophone made to squawk like a child. How I hankered after learning how to play one."

"Why didn't you take lessons?" Fanny asks.

"Lessons cost money. I took roping instead, from my brother Henry. 'Roping,' our Daddy said, 'is something a person always can use.' "

Fanny has stopped eating. "Roping?" she says, surprised. It's the first time she's heard it. It's not a subject likely to come up in Tenafly. Steer are just as rare as pigs in town. Still, Hildegarde's conversation has given Fanny an idea. "What would you think of my taking tap-dancing lessons?" she asks.

"Tap dancing?" Hildegarde studies Fanny thoughtfully. "Where would you practice?" she says, trying to be tactful. "Fat people shouldn't dance," ranch hands used to say in Texas. Certainly, Hildegarde can't tell Fanny that. It wouldn't be kind. It also wouldn't be accurate. Many fat people are light on their feet. A person can be very stout and still be an excellent dancer. The question is, will Fanny be such a person?

That evening, Fanny raises the subject with her parents on

the telephone, a three-way conference call. They are both delighted. It confirms for them their early and high hopes for her. "What a good idea," they say. "Tap is coming back," they tell each other, after she's hung up.

"Where can I practice?" Fanny asks her mother the next time she comes home.

Muffin thinks for a minute. "It's no problem," she says. "Your father will build you a dance floor in the basement."

"Dance floor?" Bernie says, and looks a bit surprised when Fanny tells him. He's never been that handy. Then he says, "Sure, it's no problem. Don't worry." He arranges for a carpenter to come lay one down. Naturally, this takes a bit of time.

While the work is going on, Fanny explains her plan to Bertha. "Soon your problems will be over," she says. "I'm planning to take tap-dance lessons. Then I'll teach your brothers how. They can practice on the dance floor in my basement. When they've got their routines down, your mother can give up her jobs and be their agent."

Bertha sighs, remembering all those other lessons Fanny took.

Fanny reexamines her plan. "Well, it's just a stopgap measure," she says. "Until your father gets back."

Bertha continues to look doubtful. She still thinks seven is too young for a job. Also, she isn't certain how she'd feel to have her mother be an agent. Life is hard now, but at least she always knows where her mother is. Even so, she's reluctant to criticize. She understands that Fanny's only thinking of the Segals. Bertha also believes lessons might do Fanny some good. Fanny could use the exercise, plus they might take her mind off her problems, whatever they are.

"What's wrong with you?" Bertha sometimes asks her. "If I didn't know better, I'd think you'd lost your best friend." Fanny never says. But she looks so happy this minute about tap dancing that Bertha can't bring herself to say no.

"Sure," Bertha says. "Why not?" Besides, she tells herself, by the time the boys learn how, they'll be older than seven, and by then, our father may be back. Of course, each girl may be talking to the wrong person. Someone probably should have asked the triplets first.

Marvin, Marc, and Matthew

SEE FANNY AND BERTHA, Marvin, Marc, and Matthew. It is after school and they are on their way to Fanny's house to look at the dance floor. "It's almost finished," Fanny told Bertha that morning. "It's being sanded today." She meant smoothed. There are dancers who tap on sand, but Fanny is not planning to be one of them. Neither are the boys. They're not even planning to be dancers. No one's told them yet. They think they're only going to see Hildegarde and hear her tell them stories, as she sometimes does.

This is how they look: almost the same, but not quite. They're wearing "vintage clothing" in assorted fashion. Before their father disappeared, they often dressed alike. Then their mother bought them matching outfits in department stores.

Now Bertha is in charge of shopping. "New to You—Used Clothes Bought and Sold" reads the sign in the window of the thrift shop. "You boys just pick out what you like," Bertha tells her brothers, and they do. Ms. O'Leary, the owner, helps them find their sizes. She thinks all four children are adorable. "Though that Bertha is much too thin," she tells her husband at night.

Today, Marvin is dressed in a navy flannel shirt and white pants with navy stripes up and down each side. It's warm enough that he doesn't need a jacket. He has wrapped his favorite bandanna around his neck. It is very large and bright red. He walks briskly, with his head held high. He's almost a whole half a block in front of the others. He holds a rolled-up comic book in one hand and waves it in the air as he would a baton. He could be leading a parade. Certainly he looks dashing for a seven-year-old. Marvin takes pride in being a triplet. He loves the attention.

Marc, on the other hand, thinks life might be more rewarding as a single. "I'd like to be noticed for myself at least sometimes," he is telling Fanny this minute. He is walking alongside her, reading a book as he walks, and swinging his schoolbag. He calls it a briefcase and is seldom without it. Inside are his schoolbooks, pencils and paper, his library card, and also the leftover part of his lunch in case he gets hungry later. "Marvin is such a show-off," he says, frowning at his brother's back. Marc sees himself as a serious person and dresses accordingly. He has on a white shirt, a bit too large for him and slightly frayed, and a striped maroon-and-gray tie. Ties are definitely not required in third grade, but Marc likes to wear one anyway. His pants are dark and pleated, and his shoes are the kind that tie. "Mark my words," Ms. O'Leary tells her husband. "That boy is going to be a stockbroker one day, or a banker." Marc prides himself on his right-handedness. Both his brothers are lefties. He is grateful even just for this minor distinction.

"Hurry up, Matthew," Bertha calls back over her shoulder. Matthew, dressed in khaki-colored pants, a brown-and-white-striped T-shirt, and beat-up tennis shoes, has fallen behind. It's a wonder he can even see where he's going. He has on a white painter's hat whose brim he's pulled down almost over his eyes. Matthew is very shy. It's hard for him just to look up and say "hi." Possibly this is his natural disposition, or perhaps it comes from his being the unmatched triplet, while his brothers are true identical twins. A person would have to look hard, though, to notice. You could tell by his eyes, hazel, definitely shades lighter than his brothers'. He also has a tiny spot, hardly a mole, a beauty mark, just beneath his right earlobe. Today, he seems a smidgen taller than his brothers. By next week, though, he may be shorter. It is his spiral notebook that is the surest giveaway. He carries it with him wherever he goes. *Matthew Segal, Personal* is printed in ink on the inside front cover. Matthew writes in his book his innermost thoughts and his feelings. "I wish I were taller," he wrote in his notebook today after recess, during which he couldn't even hit the hoop, much less get the basketball to go through it.

In fact he is, this minute, taller than his brothers, but all three of them are quite short for their age. They're even shorter for third grade. That's because they ought to be in second, but they started school early.

"If the teacher asks, tell her you're six," their mother instructed them their very first day in school.

"Our mother said to say we're six, but really we're five," the boys dutifully reported to their first-grade teacher, Ms. Bonsa, when she asked them.

"I see," she said. She sent a note home to their mother asking her please to come to school for a conference.

"THEIR FATHER'S LOST," their mother told Ms. Bonsa when they met. She explained her situation. (This was before Caesar's, when even Bertha was too young to be left home evenings unsupervised.) "I have a full-time job to make ends meet," she said. "I don't get off until after two. Kindergarten's only half a day. There'd be no one home to watch the boys."

Ms. Bonsa thought it over. She was a reasonable person. "Ummm," she said. "I suppose it won't hurt to wait and see how the boys do with reading."

All three did very well. Ms. Bonsa helped them and they worked hard. Their mother helped, too, and so did Bertha, and Fanny, and even Hildegarde. "The better I read, the bigger I feel," Matthew wrote in his notebook. He also told Bertha.

"Well, sure," she said. But still she insisted on exercise. "If you want to grow tall, you have to keep stretching." She instructed the three of them.

"If you want to grow tall, you have to eat more," Fanny advised.

But Hildegarde told them, "It's all in your genes. My mother was a very tall woman, and *her* mother was gigantic." But when the triplets asked, "How tall?" Hildegarde only said, "Very tall, believe me." The triplets believed her. They still picture Hildegarde's grandmother as an elderly giant with white hair, dressed in cowgirl clothing, tooled leather boots, and a large sombrero.

All three boys love Hildegarde. They admire everything about her. They want to be like her when they grow up—over six feet tall—and speak with a drawl. They practice by saying "howdy," though it sounds a bit odd with their New Jersey accents.

"Howdy," they say this minute, as Hildegarde opens the screen door.

"Howdy, boys," she tells them back. "Hi, Fanny! Hi, Bertie!" Bertha beams. She loves being called Bertie. She hopes one day it will catch on.

"I guess you've come to check out the floor before your dancing lessons start," Hildegarde says to the triplets. So far, she's heard that much of the plan, but no more.

"It will keep the boys busy and give Bertha a chance to sit

down and rest," was what Fanny had said. It sounded fine to Hildegarde. She has no idea at all, yet, about television.

"Dancing lessons?" the boys say, horrified. It's news to them.

"I think our best bet is to introduce the idea slowly, a step at a time," Fanny had told Bertha. "A person has to get used to the idea of being a star. Believe me, once they see the dance floor, wild horses won't be able to keep them off it."

"Wild horses?" said Bertha, raising an eyebrow.

"Everyone should know how to dance, at least a little," Hildegarde tells the triplets now. "I myself know a step or two." She demonstrates by clapping her hands for a beat and moving her feet in a bit of a hoedown shuffle she learned in Texas as a child. Hildegarde is very graceful for such a tall person. "I learned from Henry, and Henry learned from our father," she says to the children. "Pa hardly came up to Ma's shoulders, but I tell you that man could dance. He could fiddle, too. Sometimes he fiddled and danced both at the same time. Ma kept him company on her ukulele. Sometimes she danced, too. You all go on down now and look at Fanny's floor. I bet once you see it, wild horses won't keep you off it. When you come back up, I'll tell you a story." The children troop downstairs. Bertha and the boys examine the floor.

"Go ahead. Take off your shoes and try it." Fanny encourages the triplets. They do. They slip and slide around it in their stockinged feet, almost like skating on ice. "See," Fanny tells

Bertha. "I told you they'd like it." Bertha only nods. She thinks sock gliding is a long way from tap dancing. She doesn't want to hurt Fanny's feelings, though, so she keeps her thoughts to herself.

One thing at least turns out true. It is hard to coax the boys off the floor and back into their shoes. It's the smell of Hildegarde's cooking that finally does it. They go upstairs and join her in the kitchen. She's frying crisp tortillas and squeezing juice from fresh papayas. Everyone sits at the table and eats. Fanny butters her tortillas and pours syrup on them. They resemble hotcakes that way. The others sprinkle theirs with cheese, roll them up, and dip them in red sauce. Only Hildegarde drinks juice. The children ask for water. Hildegarde serves it, as always, with ice cubes and a slice of lemon in each glass.

"Are you going to tell us the story now?" asks Marvin.

"About the wild horses," Marc says.

"Well, it's not really about wild horses," says Hildegarde. "Almost a wild horse. More like a burro. It happened to my father when he was your age in Texas. He had just turned seven that summer. He and his father were taking the burro to town. It was a hot day and everyone was walking. A stranger passed them by, going in the opposite direction. 'Some one of you at least ought to ride,' the stranger said. So, my granddaddy climbed onto the back of the burro, and they traveled along that way for a while. Pretty soon, though, they came upon a farmer mending a fence at the edge of his field. 'If that don't beat all,' he said, staring. 'A grown man riding and that poor little boy having to run alongside. He's only a child.' So, my granddaddy climbed down from the burro and lifted my father onto it. They went along that way until they passed an old man herding sheep. 'Imagine that,' he said. 'A lad riding while his poor old dad has to walk behind.' When my granddaddy heard that, he climbed back up onto the burro behind my daddy and all three kept on down that road. They weren't far from town when the sheriff drove by in his car, and stopped. 'You all better get down off that burro,' he said. 'It's too hot of a day for riding that way.

You want to think of that poor animal.' As my father and his father climbed off, the sheriff waved and drove away. 'Seems like we've got only one choice left,' my grandfather said. 'Someone's sure to come along and mind, but there's no such a thing as pleasing the world.' So then the two of them lifted that burro onto their shoulders and carried him aslant the rest of the way into town."

"We heard a story like that in school," says Marc.

"You heard a story in school about my daddy and granddaddy?" Hildegarde asks, sounding surprised.

"Almost like that," says Marvin.

Hildegarde seems to think it over. "Well, sure," she says in a while. "See, a good story like that you couldn't keep a secret even in Texas. Of course if it happened nowadays it would have ended somewhat differently."

"Ended how?" Matthew asks.

"Nowadays, for sure, any father and his son would just have gone back home, picked up the van, put the burro in it, then hauled him into town. It's why my brother Henry gave up ranching and opened a garage. 'Cowboys don't ride anymore, and animals don't walk. Everybody goes by truck,' Henry says. That's what Henry does; he fixes trucks for a living."

"Is that really true?" Marvin wants to know.

"Sure," says Hildegarde. "You don't think I'd make up something like that, do you? You can go to Texas right now and see for yourself: Every day on the highway burros riding back and forth in the backs of vans, their ears stuck forward, their lips pushed back, their eyes wide open, watching all the other burros riding by."

THE FOLLOWING DAY, Fanny tells Hildegarde the rest of her plan. "So what do you think?" she asks when she's finished.

"What do I think about what?" asks Hildegarde.

"What do you think about the triplets going into show business? Won't they make an adorable act?"

Hildegarde doesn't answer right away. She's thinking how they all looked yesterday tripping over one another's feet going out the door on their way home. "Well," she says finally. "There's no question but that they're adorable. What you want to keep in mind, though, is that dancing girl and her milk pail."

"Dancing girl and her milk pail?" asks Fanny.

"Sure," says Hildegarde, and refreshes Fanny's memory. "One time a young girl came carrying her pail of milk, planning to sell it and buy eggs with the money. After her eggs hatched, she thought how she would sell the chickens and use her profits to buy herself a fancy blue-ribboned ball gown. Then she'd go to the Christmas ball, kick up her heels, and dance with the fellows. Of course, wouldn't you know, just as she was thinking this, she took a step or two by way of practice, tripped over her own two feet, and fell down. Naturally, all her milk spilled on the ground. That girl never did get her gown, at least not that year, but she did learn there's more to dancing than just knowing some steps."

38

"Are you sure you've got that story right?" Fanny asks Hildegarde. "I heard it in school, but it ended differently."

"Really," Hildegarde says, sounding interested. "How did it end?"

" 'Don't count your chickens before they're hatched.' I don't think dancing was even mentioned."

"Ah," says Hildegarde. "See, the girl in my story did everything in Texas. The girl you heard about must have come from someplace else."

Dancing Lessons

FANNY IS A STUDENT of the dance now. She takes lessons after school with Ms. Cornelius. Mondays and Fridays she has classes. Wednesdays are private. This is a lot of dancing for just a beginner; also expensive. Before she started, Fanny's parents talked it over on the telephone, long distance.

"You want to strike while the iron is hot," Bernie said.

"Right," Muffin agreed. "Besides, it's not as if we can't afford it."

Neither one has the least idea about Fanny's show-business plan, yet, but they're pleased by her commitment. They know to do something well a person has to practice. They believe in hard work.

Fanny believes in it, too, now. She sees herself as a person

with a mission. She's also in a hurry. "Time is of the essence," she tells Bertha, repeating what she's often heard at home. "Before the triplets get too old." She really means too tall, though. Fanny knows that talent counts, but being cute is also important. "Small children on stage look adorable," she tells Bertha. Well, of course they do, but having rhythm also helps.

Fanny, as it turns out, has rhythm. There she is in dance class now, third row from the front, and second from the left. She is right behind the tall girl with red braids, freckles, and eyeglasses. All the children have on leotards and tights.

Fanny made quite a stir when she first showed up in class. She was wearing bright red sweats, navy socks, and black tap shoes. "Any baggy clothes are fine for practice," she'd read in the book she borrowed from the public library, *The Beginner's Guide to Tap Dance*.

"Not in my class," Ms. Cornelius said. Now Fanny dresses the same as all the others. She doesn't do it in the dressing room, though. Instead, she wears her regular clothes over her dance clothes going back and forth to school. It's true this makes her look a tiny bit chubbier than usual, but Fanny already knows about changing clothes in front of other children from gym. Then she has no choice.

"Any child I find wearing her gym uniform underneath her school clothes will get an automatic F for the day," the gym teacher, Ms. Gilchrist, regularly warns her classes. "It's unhygienic and unhealthy. It's how you catch colds. You also smell like baby goats in gym clothes."

Fanny, shuffling in time now, smiles. She pictures to herself a herd of kids, with smooth coats and short tails, kicking up their heels. All of them are dressed in gym bloomers.

Fanny's thoughts are interrupted by Ms. Cornelius, who is calling out instructions to the class. "Eyes front! Heads up! Listen to the music!" The children flap and shuffle, brush and turn, huffing and puffing, trying to keep up with the piano. Fanny flaps and shuffles, too. But she is not huffing and puffing. She is dancing very gracefully, in perfect time to the beat. She looks surprisingly light on her feet.

"Fanny," Ms. Cornelius told her the previous week, after her private lesson, "I think you have a definite flair for dancing."

"Thank you," said Fanny.

"Very good, Fanny," her teacher says now, and moves her into the front row, where she can set a good example for the others. "Ready, class! Let me see you shim-sham." Ms. Cornelius marks time for them with a stick she taps against the floor. "One more Tack Annie," she tells them. "See Fanny, how she's balancing her weight correctly on the balls of her feet." Jonathan, a graceless child in the back row, giggles, carefully covering his mouth with one hand. He has very crooked teeth. Fanny wishes Ms. Cornelius would find someone else to use as an example, but even so she's pleased hearing herself praised.

The pianist stops playing.

"Class dismissed!" says Ms. Cornelius.

Fanny doesn't dawdle. She pulls chartreuse sweatpants over her leotards, changes from tap shoes to sneakers, puts on her all-weather coat, and is gone. She walks along briskly, her stomach sucked in, her head held high, swinging her dance case with just her shoes in it. When the weather is bad and Hildegarde is not otherwise engaged, she gives Fanny a ride. But generally she says, "Walking is good exercise." Well, tap is good exercise, too. Since Fanny's started lessons, she's been getting more than her share. She doesn't mind. On the long walks home she reviews her last class, and also plans the triplets' next one. Fanny looks much happier since she's taken up tap.

Bertha looks happier, too; more relaxed. She frowns much

less than she used to. At least this is true on Tuesdays and Thursdays, when the triplets go to Fanny's house for their lessons. Bertha goes too, though she doesn't dance. She stretches out on Muffin's chaise longue in the basement, and watches.

"Here, Bertie, have a snack," Hildegarde says every time. "It isn't good to be bone-thin." She feeds her foods that are at once fattening and fortifying; coconut milk, for instance, or popcorn enriched with granola. Hildegarde likes children. "It makes my heart glad, to have a basement full of them," she tells Henry in Texas.

Only the triplets look a teensy bit uneasy. They were surprised to find out how much hard work dancing is. "Reading is a snap next to tap," Matthew wrote in his notebook after just the first week. Even so, all three look adorable, dressed as they are for their lesson.

They have borrowed their dancing clothes from Bertha, and from their father's wardrobe. "It's not as if Pop needs them this minute," Marc told Marvin and Matthew, selecting several shirts from the rack. All their outfits have this in common: tucked-up pants legs, rolled-up shirtsleeves, pinned-back collars, and tied-up tails. A lot of safety pins go into their attire. They pay attention, too, to details. Marvin has on today, for instance, a lavender ascot with tassels. They bounce up and down as he taps. Marc is wearing a polka-dot bow tie. "I saw a man on television tap dance in one," he explains. Matthew has on his favorite fisherman's cap. "How can he see where he's dancing?" Hildegarde asks Fanny. Fanny shrugs. She believes dressing up is the boys' main reason for going along with her plan, which by now she has revealed to them.

Fanny is dressed up, too. She thinks the teacher, at least, should look professional. She has on black tights and leotards, over which she has pulled a baggy yellow sweatshirt, borrowed from Hildegarde, and red wool leg-warmers. There is considerable overlap in the vicinity of her knees.

Fanny's shoes are by Capezio, black patent leather with heels, ties, and adjustable taps. The boys admire them and want some, too. But tap shoes are expensive. They dance, instead, in their house slippers. "It's called soft shoe," Fanny tells them. "Don't worry," she adds. "It's only temporary." She and Bertha have a plan. They worked it out with Ms. O'Leary in the thrift shop.

"Tap, you don't say?" Ms. O'Leary said when they first approached her. "I was a bit of a dancer myself when I was their age. Step dancer. We did it in clogs. We put copper pennies on the heels to get the right sound." Then Ms. O'Leary stood tall, straightened her arms at her sides somewhat stiffly, lifted her knees, and tapped her feet smartly on the wooden floor in the thrift shop to show the girls how. "I'll keep my eyes out for tap shoes," she told them. "Sooner or later, they're bound to turn up. Everything does. The size won't matter. What you'll want to do is remove the taps and take them to the shoeman. He can nail them onto the boys' Sunday shoes."

"That should get them some attention walking into church," Hildegarde says when they tell her. As if they don't get plenty now.

"I'll lay out the money, whatever it comes to. I'll start saving my allowance. The boys can pay me back when they get famous," Fanny says. In the meantime, she has used her last few weeks' allowance to buy tap-dance records for practice. She turns one on now.

"Okay, boys," she sings out. "Pull up your socks and let's get down to it."

The boys look at one another and giggle. "Five, six, seven, eight." Fanny chants, clapping her hands and tapping her feet in time to the beat. The boys moan and mumble, groan and grumble, as they try to follow her lead.

"Can we take five?" Marvin asks every few minutes.

"I don't think we're cut out to be dancers," Marc says.

"I think we're too short," says Matthew.

"Don't be silly," Fanny tells them. "Ida Forsyne was much shorter than you, and she was famous. She was a child star. She was so short that even after she grew up, she never wore larger than a size-two tap shoe. If she could do it, so can you."

"Well, sure," says Marc. "But there was only one of her. I think working with three it's much harder."

"Hard?" says Fanny, and turns off the music. "Okay, boys, take five," she says. "I'll tell you about hard." They all flop down on the floor; the regular floor, not the dance one. No one wants splinters.

"What you're doing is easy," Fanny says. "It's nothing. It's a piece of cake. You take Cathy Harris, now. What she did was hard." Fanny knows about her, the same as Ida, from her dance book. The boys, of course, have never heard of her, but they're willing to listen. They think anything would be more interesting than having to shuffle, hop, and tap even one more time.

"Cathy Harris," Fanny tells them, "was a thin and delicate child. She was probably your same age when she took up tapping. She did it on the advice of her doctor. He hoped it would improve her health. Cathy turned out to have an aptitude for it. She became a world-class dancer. She traveled to near and faraway places with her mother, making money tapping. Her specialty was acrobatic tap on ice. She did back flips, hand springs, round-offs, nip-ups. She wore nails on the soles of her tap shoes to keep her from slipping. What Cathy did was truly difficult. Also dangerous. Cathy's mother sat in the audience every time Cathy performed, watching and praying. See, all you boys have to do is shuffle, hop, step in time, and remember your combinations.

"Let's take it from the top now," Fanny says, and turns the record back on. She calls out advice. "Syncopate your feet, please. Let me see you slide." The triplets try. "Try harder," Fanny says, and worries that they're only going through the motions to get by. Matthew looks especially preoccupied. He wants to know more about Cathy. Was her doctor right? Did dancing make her strong and sturdy? He wishes Fanny had finished her story.

Hildegarde comes down the stairs to watch. She can hardly believe what she sees. Each triplet is out of step in his own way. For all the good it's doing, there might as well not even be a record playing. You would think, she thinks, that even just by accident two of them would wind up on the same foot at the same time every now and then. But as far as she can tell, it hasn't happened yet. Fanny, on the other hand, is dancing fine.

"Can I speak to you frankly?" Hildegarde asks Fanny after Bertha and the boys have gone home.

"Sure," Fanny says. "What's up?"

"You've turned into a very good dancer," Hildegarde tells her. "I wish my brother Henry could see you."

"Thank you," says Fanny.

"On the other hand . . ." Hildegarde goes on. "I think for you to buy taps for the boys would be a waste of good money. I don't think taps are your problem."

"Oh?" says Fanny.

"See, some people have it in them to be dancers, and some people have it in them to be other things."

"Like what?" Fanny asks.

"Take your pick," says Hildegarde. "There's plenty of choices. Painting, for instance, or music, French, cooking, tennis, architecture, auto mechanics." Hildegarde knows about all these things from television. She watches the educational channel while Fanny's in school, and pays attention.

Fanny isn't convinced, though. She knows from experience, and also from her parents, the importance of practice. "If you can walk you can dance," she tells Hildegarde, quoting from her dance book.

"You don't say," says Hildegarde. She seems to think about it. "I've seen possums walk in Texas," she says after a while. "Also an armadillo or two in my time. Funny thing, I've never seen one dancing."

"Ummm," says Fanny. She's not about to give up her plan so quickly. She decides to talk it over with her mother and ask for her advice. If anyone would know, Muffin should. It's her job after all.

"I'd like your professional opinion," Fanny says to her mother that night. Muffin is pleased to be asked. She adjusts her appointments schedule slightly, so as to be at home for the triplets' next lesson.

"I'VE SET UP an audition," Fanny tells the boys on Tuesday, right before they start warming up. "Don't be nervous. It's just my mom coming to watch."

The triplets are nervous. After they've had time to practice, Fanny calls to her mom: "We're ready whenever you are." Muffin comes partway downstairs and sits on a step. She sees Bertha stretched out in the chaise longue, eating. Muffin doesn't mind, though she hopes Bertha won't leave any crumbs. She's thinking of wildlife. Several months before she came downstairs to the laundry room in search of fresh underwear. She saw a furry creature asleep in her chair. Muffin had turned around quickly then, shut her eyes tightly, and run back up the stairs, empty-handed, making little gasping noises all the way. She arrived in the kitchen just as Hildegarde and Fanny were finishing their breakfasts. "There's a small furry creature in the basement," Muffin said, panting, "and it's sleeping in my chaise longue." Hildegarde went to look.

"It's just a mouse," she said, returning. Later that day she caught it in a bucket and released it in some woods. Muffin, however, gave up using her chaise altogether, and now comes downstairs only when it's necessary. But first, she turns on the master switch to flood the basement with light, counts to ten, and calls loudly, "Here I come; I'm coming now." Then she clumps down the steps noisily, hoping in that way to frighten any little thing that may be lurking there.

Today, of course, such precautions aren't necessary. The room's already lit, and there's sufficient clumping going on. Muffin puts on her eyeglasses for distance. "I'm ready whenever you are," she says.

Fanny turns on the music. "Five, six, seven, eight," she says, clapping, and she and the boys begin their routine. Muffin watches carefully. She is surprised and pleased to see what a good dancer Fanny is. The boys, of course, are another story. Muffin watches quietly and claps politely when they finish. Marvin finishes first and bows with a flourish. He has wrapped a scarf, like a turban, all around his head. He only needs an earring, Muffin thinks, and he could pass for a pirate. Marc finishes next and bobs his head slightly. He's wearing his father's old tails, tucked up, and a bow tie. Cute, Muffin thinks. A bit like a penguin. Matthew finishes last. The only sign he gives of being through is when his feet stop moving. He continues to watch them, though, as if for cues. Today he's wearing a cowboy hat, slightly used and much too large. Muffin wonders how he sees with so much brim in his eyes.

"Take five, boys," Fanny says, and climbs the stairs to join her mother. The boys, breathing hard, toss themselves across Bertha's legs on the chaise.

"Fanny darling, you danced divinely," her mother says. "I always knew you had talent."

"Thank you," says Fanny. "What about the boys?"

"Ummm," says her mother. She wants to be tactful. Still, she knows as an agent, honesty is the best policy. She smiles brightly in the direction of the triplets. "They certainly are adorable," she says in a loud voice. Then she lowers it. "But dancers they're not," she adds. Talent agents spend years practicing to be heard. Even whispering, Muffin's voice carries. The triplets can hear every word. They don't mind. Isn't that what they've been saying all along? They poke one another and giggle. Bertha doesn't mind, either. She still thinks they're too young to have jobs. Also, she would not care to see her brothers travel so much, like that poor Cathy Harris with all those nails in her shoes.

MUCH LATER, that evening, before Fanny goes to bed, her mother looks at her and says, "Fanny, I think you are growing." Muffin turns toward Hildegarde. "What do you think?" she asks her. "Doesn't Fanny look taller to you?"

"Thinner," says Hildegarde, who measures Fanny monthly with pencil marks against the wall. "It's all that dancing she's been doing. Lose a few pounds, it makes you look taller." Well, sure it does. Of course, in Fanny's case, it's more than just

dancing. There are all those long walks back and forth to dancing school, not to mention running up and down the basement steps. Then, too, there's this: between buying dance records and saving for taps, Fanny's become dependent on Hildegarde for her snacks. "No, thank you," she regularly says to offers of carrot sticks, celery, and cottage-cheese dip.

Upstairs in her room, Fanny looks at herself in the mirror. She hums a few bars, takes a few steps, completes a few turns. See Fanny dancing, how gracefully she moves. It's more than being thinner; she's gained that lovely confidence one gets from doing something well. It only goes so far, though. Afterward, in her bed, tucked under the covers, she thinks of her family's affairs, and considers her parents' secret. It's a very stupid secret, she thinks, and it isn't even mine. One of these days, I'm going to tell Bertha. One of these days, I just may tell everyone.

Sponge Fishing

JUST BECAUSE YOU HOPE and expect something to happen doesn't mean you aren't surprised when it finally does. Bertha and her brothers are certainly surprised that Saturday morning when the telegram arrives. Their mother might have been surprised, too, but she is upstairs taking a bubble bath. It's her one weekend off for the month.

Marvin is first at the window, peering out, after the doorbell rings. "There's a man outside," he reports to Bertha. "He's dressed in a uniform. He's holding a clipboard." Marvin knows better than to open the door to a stranger. Anything can happen. Bertha comes and looks out over his shoulder. First she sees the man. Then she sees his van parked in the driveway. Both have writing on them.

"It's Western Union," she says, and opens the door.

"Is this the Segal residence?" the messenger asks.

Bertha says, "Yes." The triplets, all three crowded behind her now, nod. The man's jaw drops. He blinks, then shakes his head. You'd think he'd never seen triplets before. Surely he's heard of them.

"Is there something wrong with your phone?" he asks Bertha. "Usually we call." He sounds somewhat put out, almost as though he's blaming her for taking him out of the office.

"It's disconnected," Bertha tells him. "You could have phoned next door and left a message with one of the neighbors." She means with the Murgatroyds or the Delaneys. It's an arrangement they insist on. "That's what neighbors are for," both families say.

Ms. Segal is glad for their help, but warns her children. "Only in a pinch," she tells them. Of course, to leave a message a person first needs to know about the plan, and also at least one of the numbers. The children's father doesn't. Why would he? Before he disappeared, the Segals' phone worked fine.

"Sign on line nine," the messenger tells Bertha, holding out his clipboard. Bertha signs. He hands her an envelope, then rushes off. He seems in quite a hurry. He's anxious, in fact, to get back to his van and check out his vision. The first thing he does once he's in it, before he even turns on the engine, is hold up both hands and count what he sees, once with his right eye, once with his left, and once with both of them wide open. "Nothing wrong here," he says to himself, relieved to see that he still has his same ten fingers and that both his eyes are in working order.

Bertha holds the telegram up to the light, trying to read the message inside. The envelope's addressed to "The Segals."

"That's us," says Marc.

"Is it from Daddy?" asks Matthew.

"Aren't you going to open it?" Marvin wants to know.

Bertha thinks it over. Their mother had been quite specific. "Please don't anybody interrupt me until I'm finished with my bath," she'd told them. Bertha stands at the foot of the stairs and hears splashing. Well, I guess that's that, she tells herself, unsealing the envelope, removing the paper inside, and reading the message aloud:

> "EUREKA!! I'M FOUND.
> I'M COMING HOME.
> I'LL FILL IN ALL THE DETAILS
> WHEN I GET THERE.
> I'LL SEE YOU TOMORROW FOR SUPPER.
> LOVE, DAD."

The telegram is dated Friday. "Daddy's coming home tonight," Bertha says, then races up the stairs. She bangs on the bathroom door, underneath which steam is escaping, and shouts the good news to her mother. Right away, she hears the sound that water makes when it's draining from the tub.

A few minutes later, Ms. Segal is standing in the kitchen, dripping water, waving the telegram in one hand. "Didn't I always say one day your father would come back?" Considering the circumstances, she appears fairly calm. She has taken the time to put on a striped terry-cloth bathrobe that belongs to her husband. She's fastened it about herself securely with an over-size belt from Bertha's closet. She's carefully put up her hair to dry, Turkish style, in a red-and-white beach towel. Only the puddles forming at her feet show how fast she hurried from her tub down the stairs in order to read the telegram for herself.

"What we want to do first is make a list," she tells the children now.

Bertha gets paper and a pencil and writes down what her mother says: clean the house, take out the trash, buy groceries for dinner, cook, everybody bathed and dressed. Well, Ms. Segal has just finished bathing, but she knows how dirty a person can get doing housework. She plans to look her best when her husband gets back from wherever he's been.

There's something she's left off her list. The triplets confer with one another while cleaning their room. Then, while their mother's cooking dinner, they put all their father's clothes they've borrowed back into his dresser drawers and closet.

"That's that," Marc says, brushing the palms of his hands together.

"It's not as if we need them anymore," says Marvin.

"I think our dancing days are numbered," Matthew writes, later, in his notebook.

It isn't clear whether the boys have in mind just their father's homecoming, or also their audition at Fanny's last week.

BY LATE AFTERNOON, everything is ready. Ms. Segal's list is all crossed off. The house is clean and filled with the aromas of cooking. Chicken stew with pineapple sauce is simmering on the stove top, and biscuits made from scratch are ready for the oven. The children are dressed in their best clothes, carefully layered to hide the worn spots. Ms. Segal has put on a yellow

59

silk kimono, saved from better days for a special occasion. She's pulled back her dark hair with a wide blue ribbon. Bertha has set up two checkerboards on the sofa and she and her brothers are playing, looking out the window for their father between every move. That is why they're first to see the taxicab as it turns into their driveway and stops. They watch as their father climbs out, a single duffel bag in one hand. He pays the driver.

"Daddy's here," Bertha shouts to her mother in the kitchen. He certainly looks different from how she remembers him. For one thing, he has a beard. Also, he's definitely much thinner, and very suntanned.

"Daddy looks taller, doesn't he?" Marc says to anyone.

"He's barefoot," says Marvin.

"He is not either," Matthew says. "He has on sandals." He's also wearing dungarees. Bertha is amazed. Before he went away he never went outside except in a three-piece suit, a starched shirt, and a tie.

Before the children can discuss their father further, their mother has thrown open the door and herself into his arms. He isn't even inside the house yet and they're kissing in the doorway. The children have never seen such goings-on, excepting perhaps in the movies. They themselves hang back from sudden shyness. But then their parents separate and it is their turn. "It is so good to be home," their father keeps saying. "I can't believe how the children have grown." All the while, he's picking up this one and putting down that one, and running his

hands over somebody's hair, hugging and squeezing and kissing. You can just imagine the excitement. They all have waited for this moment such a long time.

"DINNER," their mother finally announces, brushing back the hair that's escaped from her ribbon. Her cheeks are rather flushed. It would be hard to say with certainty from what. It could be from pure happiness, or her husband's new beard, or just the warm steam from the stew pot over which she was standing. Most likely, it's some combination. In any event, it's very becoming.

"So," she says, once everyone's seated and the food has been served. "Tell us everything. We want all the details." She looks at her husband expectantly. The children do, too. They all want to know where he's been and what he's done and seen since the day his plane disappeared.

Their father looks at them and shrugs. "There's not *that* much to tell," he says, and sounds peculiarly perplexed. "There are hardly any details. See, all this time I've had amnesia."

"Amnesia?" echoes Bertha's mother. Her echo seems to float around the dinner table.

"I've been cleaning sponges for over two years," says Mr. Segal. "In a little hut on an island off the coast of Florida."

Cleaning sponges? Matthew would like to interrupt, but doesn't. His father continues with his story.

"All I could remember all that time was a small private

plane on its way to Bermuda. Only I and the pilot and one other passenger were aboard. A sudden storm came up. 'No problem,' said the pilot. 'There's plenty of islands below a small plane can land on.' The next thing I knew, I was in the water by myself clinging for dear life to a floating coconut tree. My clothing was all gone, except for my underwear, which I still had on. Fortunately, the water is warm down there. Unfortunately, I had nothing with which to crack open a coconut. I wasn't cold when I was rescued, but believe me I was hungry.

"Hector Roberto Ortiz was my savior, a sponge fisherman who found me, put me in his boat, and took me back with him to his home in the Florida Keys. My mind was a total blank. I didn't even remember my name. 'Don't worry,' said Mr. Ortiz. 'Be glad you're alive. You're only speaking English so you must be North American. I'll just call you Jack until your memory comes back. It's easy to remember.' "

"Jack?" Bertha's mother says, looking carefully at her husband. She herself prefers more syllables in a name. Bertha, though, likes how modern it sounds; so different from Simon, her father's first name when he left.

"I went to work for him. Mr. Ortiz is proprietor of the largest sponge market on the East Coast," Bertha's father explains. "But he sells more than just sponges. He carries everything to do with the sea: scuba and snorkeling and boating equipment, collectors' shells, sea horses, sundries; sometimes he finds pearls, strings them, and sells them. He taught me the cleaning end of the business. 'You seem to have a flair for this,' he said. 'Perhaps in your former life you did something like it.' Who knew? I was in no position to contradict. I hadn't a clue to my former life, who I was, or what I did. It wasn't a bad way of life down there either, except I always felt something was missing."

"I should say so," Bertha's mother says. "We were missing. Didn't you ever once think of us, and worry about how we were doing?"

Bertha's father looks surprised. "How could I?" he asks. "Don't you see, all I could remember of my life was after I was found. Are you forgetting that I had amnesia? Believe me, it was awful. I didn't know my name. I had no relatives, no birth certificate, no bank account, no driver's license, not even a social security number or a passport. 'Don't worry,' Mr. Ortiz kept telling me. 'One day, just like that, all your memories will come back.' Even that worried me. Suppose I'd been an ax murderer in my former life. I could have been escaping on the plane from federal prison, or from a lunatic asylum. 'Escapees get found,' Mr. Ortiz told me. 'I don't see anyone looking for you.' "

Matthew, who has listened patiently until now, interrupts. "Excuse me," he says. "I know about sponges *for* cleaning, but I have never heard of anybody cleaning *them*."

"Right," says his father. "I once thought that, too. But see, here's what you do. First you have to fetch the sponges from the ocean floor. You go out in a boat along the shore where the water is shallow, and use long poles with hooks on the ends. You take the sponges back, clean out the seashells, seaweed, all the debris that isn't bony skeleton. Then you hang them up to dry. Afterward, you sort and grade, then wrap and sell them. Some people dive for them instead of using poles. But I had no idea if I knew how to dive. I did know I could swim from all that time I'd spent in the water, just me and the coconut tree."

"Is it nice in Florida?" the children ask.

"Sure it's nice. Sunny days, long warm nights, lots of stars, and plenty of seafood free for the catching. Well, there are a few bad things: too many tourists in winter, too hot in summer, so many alligators to look out for."

"Alligators?" the triplets say all together.

"Sure. Alligators like warm weather and seafood. They like tourists, too. A person has to remember to steer clear of them. Now and then, someone forgets. Usually someone on the lookout for buried treasure. A person with his mind set on gold, I guess, is liable to forget about the alligators lurking in the swamps."

"Buried treasure?" says Marc.

"Left over from the pirates." His father explains: "Galleons were sunk off the coast, long ago. Whole ships went down. Pirate crews robbed one another and buried their bounty. Lots of treasure was never dug up. It's still there for the taking. Of course, you want to be careful.

"One time, a boy from the next island over went looking for treasure and forgot to be careful. This was before my time, but I heard all about it. Unfortunately, before that boy could find his treasure, an alligator found him. Fortunately, a tree was nearby. The boy was an excellent climber and shinnied right up it. An alligator, of course, can't climb a tree. Its legs are too short. It will, however, wait patiently at the bottom. It knows, sooner or later, a person is bound to come down. Fortunately for the boy, he had his harmonica with him. Stuck up there in that tree as he was, he removed it from his pocket and began to play it. He did so to pass the time, and also to calm himself. He'd begun to feel rather nervous. It seems to have calmed the alligator, too, who apparently liked harmonica music. At least, it put its head to one side and listened. After a while, its head began nodding and the alligator fell asleep. Right away, the boy stopped playing and began to climb down the tree. Unfortunately, as soon as the music stopped, the alligator woke up. It isn't easy to climb down a tree playing a harmonica as you go, especially when the tree is so tall and so straight as that tree was, with hardly any branches. Eventually, though, the boy must have figured out some way, or at least he was very persistent, because he did get home the next day to tell his story. He kept on telling it, too. He'd also learned his lesson.

"Afterward, whenever he went treasure hunting, he took his harmonica along, plus some other person. That way, they could take turns if they had to: one could play while the other climbed down, one could climb down while the other one played, until both were safely on the ground and on their way home, and the alligator still sound asleep."

Mr. Segal stops talking. He looks around the table, and smiles at his family. He seems very happy to be home himself. His family, of course, is happy, too, to have him back. Still, they have some questions.

"So," Ms. Segal asks. "What made you give up sponges and come home?" Mr. Segal looks surprised. Hasn't she been listening?

"I came back as soon as I could," he says. "The second I knew who I was, I began to make plans. This was how that happened: Almost every day after work, I'd walk along the pier, look at the sunset, and try to remember my former life. There

were always crowds of tourists there. They came for the view and the free entertainment. Well, I say free, but after each act the performers pass a hat, hoping the tourists will put money into it. There are jugglers there, and clowns, trained cats, some contortionists from India. I always hoped someone who knew me from before would see and recognize me there, but no one ever did. Then, just yesterday, I saw a new act: boy triplets doing acrobatics on the boardwalk with their father. They did flips and cartwheels, shoulder stands and backbends. Some tricks they did holding sticks in their mouths with plates balanced on the ends. They were really something to behold. In between tricks, they did a little soft shoe. The boys were just about your same age," Mr. Segal says, pausing to look around the table at his own three sons. Then he goes on. "As I stood there watching, I heard myself say, half to myself and half aloud, 'I'm certainly glad my boys are at home doing schoolwork, and not outside doing tricks on some boardwalk.' Then, just like that, out of the blue, my whole life came back to me. I remembered all of you and knew what I'd been missing. I tried to telephone but couldn't reach you. So, I bought an airplane ticket home and sent a telegram instead. The next morning, I thanked Mr. Ortiz and hugged him good-bye. Now, here I am back in Tenafly. The rest is history. It's your turn now. Tell me everything that's happened since I've been gone."

Ms. Segal feels herself close to speechless. She sits back in her chair and lets the children talk. They take turns filling in the details. They tell their father everything.

"You've certainly all been busy," he says when they finish. "I see I wasn't the only one kicking just to keep my head above water. Imagine, all that basement dancing, TV planning, so much cooking. No wonder you all look pale. Plus, Bertha's too thin. She needs to put on a few pounds." Well, lately she's begun to, eating Hildegarde's snacks on the chaise longue as she watches her brothers dance—but her father wouldn't know that. "Everyone must be very tired," he says. "I think right now we ought to go to sleep. We'll see what's what in the morning."

As the children get ready for bed, they discuss this new turn of events.

"Does Daddy seem different to you?" Marc asks.

"Different how?" says Marvin.

"He's got a beard," says Matthew. "Plus he's more sun-tanned."

"Right," says Bertha. "He's a sponge man now. It's a whole different life from military hardware; so much exercise and fresh air. You can tell; he looks more relaxed."

The triplets get into their beds. First Bertha, then both their parents, kiss them good-night. "Sleep tight," everyone says. Marvin falls asleep first. He dreams he's an acrobat in a circus. Marc falls asleep next. He dreams he owns a chain of sponge stores, and a fleet of ships. Matthew isn't *that* sleepy. He sits up in bed and writes in his notebook: "Daddy's back from Bermuda, and also from Florida. He cleaned sponges there for a living. No more military hardware. No more dancing for us, I think, either. 'My boys belong in school,' our daddy says. 'Not doing tricks on some boardwalk.' I think he also means television. I wonder how he feels about hotcakes and pizza. I wonder if Mom will keep making them. It would be nice if she could just stay home again. I wonder if Daddy will ever go back to selling backpack radios and plane parts. I think there aren't too many sponges to clean in New Jersey."

Bertha isn't that sleepy either. She's hungry. She goes back downstairs to the kitchen, takes a chicken wing from the refrigerator, and eats it, cold. She washes it down with a glass of apple cider, then chews on a graham cracker. "Daddy's really back," she says to herself. She can hardly wait to see Fanny's face when she tells her the good news. Won't Fanny be surprised? she thinks. Neither girl knows it, yet, but Fanny's about to have some news of her own.

Water Witching and a Riverboat

"OUR FATHER'S BACK. He had amnesia." Bertha and the triplets tell Fanny their news. It's Monday morning, and they're standing in the school yard, talking. Sunday was spent with family.

"That's wonderful," Fanny says, referring to the first part only. She's a bit breathless from running. Having overslept, she'd got a late start. Their conversation is interrupted by the school bell. They continue it at lunch.

"He was clinging to a coconut tree by the skin of his fingers when Mr. Ortiz found him," Marvin says. Marc tells about the pirate treasure, and the Florida Keys.

"Crocodiles live there," he says.

"Alligators." Matthew corrects him.

Bertha explains about the boardwalk, and how her father's memory came back. That reminds the triplets.

"No more dancing," Marvin tells Fanny.

"Our father doesn't approve," says Marc.

Matthew nods in confirmation.

Fanny is speechless for a while. Then she says, "Well, I guess there's no point crying over spilled milk. It's a good thing we didn't buy your taps yet." If she's facing disappointment, she doesn't show it. In fact, she can hardly wait now for school to be over so she can hurry home and tell Hildegarde the news. First, though, she has dance class; and even after it, she's momentarily delayed.

"Fanny," Ms. Cornelius says. "I'd like a word with you."

"Yes?" Fanny says, as she pulls her outer clothes on over her leotards. She's alone in the room with Ms. Cornelius. The other children have gone off to get dressed, and the piano player is taking a break. What Ms. Cornelius says next takes Fanny by surprise. She beams at her teacher, then smiles all the way home. "Monday must be my good news day," she tells herself. "Hey, guess what!" she calls out to Hildegarde as she walks in through the front doorway. Hildegarde looks up from what she's doing, filling in a crossword puzzle, and frowns.

"Hay is for horses," she says.

Fanny's heard this before. "So?" she once asked.

"Sew, stitch," Hildegarde answered. This time, Fanny just waits.

"You were saying?" Hildegarde asks her politely in another minute.

Fanny tells her all she knows about Mr. Segal's homecoming. She doesn't leave out any parts, including pirate treasure, alligators, outdoor acrobats, and Mr. Segal's amnesia.

"I'm not surprised," Hildegarde says when Fanny is finished. Whether she's referring to the last part only, or the rest of it as well, isn't clear.

"How do you think treasure hunters know where to start digging for gold in the first place?" Fanny asks Hildegarde later that day.

"Witch hazel," Hildegarde answers.

"I beg your pardon?" says Fanny, politely.

Hildegarde explains. She knows about such things from her own aunt Emma. "My aunt Emma was a water witch in Texas," she says. "She used a forked stick called a divining rod. Now, some dowsers use sticks made of willow or peach, black haw or walnut. But my aunt Emma, who was one of the best, always used witch hazel. She'd walk along behind it, holding onto one branch of the forked end with each hand and pointing the other, unforked end down toward the ground. She'd go along this way until the stick began to bob. Sometimes it bobbed up and down so hard, it was all she could do to hold on. Then she knew she was onto something. 'You might as well go ahead and put your well there,' she'd tell this farmer or that one. Of course, she wasn't right every time. Sometimes a person would dig down and find gold instead, or maybe oil. So far as I know, no one ever complained. Well, Aunt Emma wasn't that pleased. 'I'm a water witch, not a doodlebugger,' she'd say those times. That's what oil finders were called. I've never known why."

"What were treasure hunters called?" Fanny asks.

Hildegarde gives her a peculiar look. "Treasure hunters," she says. "What else would they be called?" Then she goes on with her story. "One time my aunt Emma had an experience similar to that boy's with the lizard in Florida," she says.

"Alligator," says Fanny. "I didn't know there were any in Texas."

"Maybe a few," says Hildegarde. "Though it's true, they're not plentiful. It was a panther in my aunt Emma's case. It turned out a good thing for her that she'd brought my daddy's fiddle that time and could play it."

"Did she climb a tree?" Fanny asks.

"A tree wasn't even in the picture," says Hildegarde. "In the first place, it could be hard just to find one in Texas. And in the second place, a panther isn't like an alligator, waiting patiently at the bottom. Every panther born knows how to climb a tree. What happened was this: My aunt Emma had been out dowsing all day without any luck. It was just coming on dark when she heard that panther scream. Now, a panther's scream is a powerful sound. Hair-raising, especially when you're out by yourself after sundown. 'It curdled my blood,' Aunt Emma said whenever she told us the story. Lighting a fire was the first thing she did. Panthers don't much care for flames. The next thing she did was take Daddy's fiddle out of its case, position it under her chin, pick up the bow, and start playing. She played 'The Yellow Rose of Texas.' It was the only tune she knew. The sound of music always made her feel braver, Aunt Emma said. The panther must have liked it, too. At least he stopped screaming and stayed where he was, on top of the ridge of some mountain. Eventually, though, he must have got bored. Well, it was just that one tune she knew, played over and over. Aunt Emma said she was getting pretty bored herself by the time that panther gave up listening. He just loped away, peaceful-like, in perfect time to the music, was what Aunt Emma always claimed. After that, she taught herself a few more tunes, and any time she went out dowsing she took along my daddy's fiddle and her sister. That way, if the occasion arose and they had to, Aunt Emma could fiddle, while her sister, my aunt Grace, went ahead with the fire."

"It's an interesting story," Fanny tells Hildegarde when she's finished. "Thank you for telling it to me." Fanny's made up her mind. She's decided to save her second piece of news to tell her mother first when she gets home that evening.

"Hey, Mom. Guess what!" Fanny calls out the minute Muffin walks through the doorway. Hildegarde is off for the evening.

"What?" Muffin answers, setting down her briefcase, kicking off her shoes, removing her suit jacket, and sitting herself on the sofa, tucking up her feet.

"I'm dancing a solo in June at Ms. Cornelius's recital. 'Thanks for the Buggy Ride' is the name of my dance. She asked me today after class. 'Yes,' I said. 'I'd like to.' 'Fine,' she said. 'You'll need a costume with fringes and chaps, and white patent boots with adjustable taps.' I told her I didn't think that would be a problem."

"Well, of course it isn't, Fanny darling," Muffin says. "Imagine, dancing a solo. What wonderful news." Muffin could not be more pleased for her child. Also, it confirms what she has always said: Fanny has talent. Muffin sits up straighter and puts her feet on the floor. Already, she looks much less tired than when she walked through the doorway.

"Will you come?" Fanny asks her.

"With bells on," her mother answers, an old show-business expression. "I wouldn't miss it for the world." Nor would she. She gets up and goes to her desk, and circles the date Fanny tells her on her calendar in red. "We'll circle all our calendars," she says. She means, beside her own, also Fanny's, Hildegarde's, and Bernie's.

"I have more news, too," Fanny adds. "It's about Mr. Segal." She hurries on to tell it. "He's come back. It turns out, all this time he's had amnesia. He's been living off the coast of Florida until now, cleaning sponges. He didn't even know his name. People there just called him Jack." Fanny skips over the middle part of the story, about hunting for treasure, and ends with the acrobatic triplets and how their appearance caused Mr. Segal's memory to return.

"I see," says Fanny's mother. "I'm sure his family's glad he's recovered." Though Muffin is pleased for Fanny's friends' sake, she thinks it's the most farfetched story she has ever heard. But she keeps this thought to herself. Fanny keeps the rest of the story to *her*self. Muffin has begun to look tired again. Fanny thinks she's probably not up to hearing the part about the alligator. Fanny is right. Muffin's in the wrong frame of mind for so many happy endings. She's just had some news of her own that disturbs her.

"I BOUGHT A BOAT," Bernie told her earlier that day, at lunch.

"A boat?" Muffin said, as though perhaps she'd heard him wrong.

"A houseboat on the Hudson," he replied. "I'm moving into it on Sunday. I plan to be a live-aboard. I've always wanted to try life on the river."

"Really," said Muffin, wondering why he'd never mentioned it before. She was shocked to find out he'd taken such a big step without consulting her. She did realize, of course, that since their divorce Bernie was a free agent. Still, after so many years, one would think at least he'd have asked her opinion. She pushed aside the snails she was eating.

"Boats are damp," she told him. "Your clothes will get mildewed. Your books will get ruined. Not to mention, there's such a thing as rheumatism. Besides, how will you get your mail?"

"Same as now," said Bernie. "What isn't sent to the office will still get delivered. I've got a slip in a marina: The 79th Street Boat Basin, Riverside Park, New York, N.Y. Fanny can visit me there and sleep over. There's plenty of room."

"Well, sure; room," Muffin said, though in fact she was doubtful. The biggest boat she'd ever been on was a rowboat. It was also true Fanny could swim, having been twice to summer camp. But surely more things than that needed to be considered. Muffin's train of thought was interrupted by Bernie.

"So, it's settled then; you'll tell her for me? I'll be in Hollywood the rest of the week. It's not something I want to discuss on the phone. And, anyway, I think a mother knows best what to say in such cases."

Muffin was speechless.

"Thank you," Bernie said. He put the bill on his charge card, patted Muffin on the shoulder, and left. Muffin finished her snails. Then she ordered pie à la mode for dessert. She ate it thoughtfully, and wondered what to say to Fanny. . . .

She wonders now. Fanny looks so happy, twirling about in the living room, showing off her dance steps. Muffin decides to wait until morning to tell her. She feels her own evening is already ruined. Why spoil Fanny's? Muffin, of course, is aware that Fanny may not see it her way. Fanny tends to look on the bright side. She may not mind change. Besides, for all Muffin knows, Fanny may harbor secret hopes, the same as her father's, of weekends spent on a riverboat.

After Fanny has kissed her good-night and gone upstairs to bed, Muffin goes into the kitchen, gets herself a large bag of peanuts, and takes them back with her to the sofa. She sits with her feet up and starts to shell and eat the peanuts. Muffin feels confused by such a sudden turn in events. She needs time to adjust to a new situation. She wishes she could talk it over with someone she trusts, someone older; her mother for instance. But how can she? Muffin's mother doesn't even know about her divorce. Muffin looks rather sad, sitting by herself, eating peanuts and trying to decide what to do. By the time the last peanut has been shelled and eaten, Muffin has made up her mind. She picks up the telephone and calls her mother, Fanny's grandmother, in Vermont.

"Hi, Mommy," she says. "It's Marilyn." She uses her given name and not the nickname Bernie gave her. "Muffin?" her mother had said the first time she heard it. "What's wrong with the nice name we gave you?"

"I'm calling," Muffin tells her mother now, "to invite you and Daddy to Fanny's dance recital. She's doing a solo. It's the last weekend in June. You can stay here with us if you'd like. We've plenty of room."

Muffin's voice floats up the stairs. Fanny, lying in bed, but not yet asleep, can hear her quite clearly. "Fanny has turned into *some* dancer," her mother says in a proud voice. "I just

wish you could see her. Well," she adds, "in June you will. You'll hardly recognize her when you do. She's lost her baby fat. She looks so svelte and grown-up now."

Svelte? Fanny thinks. She stretches on her back in her bed and touches one hand to her stomach. There's barely a bulge. It's almost flat. Fanny smiles, closes her eyes, and pictures how she'll look on stage in June. She sees herself, dressed in her costume, framed by floodlights, in white patent tap boots, fringes, and chaps, dancing in perfect time to the music. She falls asleep and dreams she's practicing her routine. She misses hearing the rest of her mother's conversation.

Muffin tells her mother everything. Once having started talking, she finds it hard to stop. It's been a long time since they've had a real conversation. Muffin's innermost thoughts all pour out.

"Are you all right?" her mother asks, when Muffin is finally finished.

"I'm fine," Muffin says. "Fanny and I both are fine. I feel much better now having talked with you." Saying it, she sees that it is so. By the time she hangs up, she feels as though a weight's been lifted from her heart. Also, she's learned some things she didn't know before, about her own great-grandparents for instance. Muffin puts on her nightclothes. Then she fixes herself a glass of warm milk, with sugar and coffee syrup in it. She carries it to bed with her, drinks it, and thinks some more about Fanny.

"FANNY DARLING," Muffin says in the morning. "I've something to tell you." They're eating breakfast together—dry toast, boiled eggs, and grapefruit juice. Hildegarde has gone jogging. Muffin has decided to start a new diet.

"Yes?" says Fanny.

"Your father bought a houseboat. He plans to live on it. He's moving in on Sunday. It's on the Hudson River in Manhattan. You can help him pack."

"A boat?" says Fanny. "Funny that he never mentioned it. Although," she adds, "the last time he was home we ate fish for dinner almost every night, and he sang sea songs."

"I see," says Muffin. "Well, he mentioned it to me, yesterday, when you were in school. The main thing is, you're not to worry. His moving out has nothing to do with you; it's just between the two of us." Fanny sighs. She's heard this part before; well, something very similar. Muffin goes on. "It's only a bus trip away. You can visit when you like and sleep over on weekends. You can invite your friends; Bertha, for instance, and those adorable triplets. Your father says there's plenty of room. There's probably also a very good view, plus all the fresh fish you can eat." Muffin wonders just then about snails, if they're a river food or some sort of land fish.

"Ummm," says Fanny. She needs time to think about this. The possibility of life on the river, even part-time, has never crossed her mind before. Muffin goes on with her end of the conversation, only seeming to veer course.

"I spoke with Grandma in Vermont last night," she says.

"She and Grandpa are planning to come to your recital and stay with us. I told her I was divorced."

Fanny swallows the wrong way and chokes on her toast. Muffin reaches over to pat her on the back. "Well, they were bound to find out," she says. "Staying over, after all, and your father on the river sleeping in a boat. Besides, they're family. It's high time they knew." Fanny takes a sip of grapefruit juice.

"What did Grandma say?" she asks.

Muffin smiles. "First, she said, 'Divorce isn't the worst thing in the world.' Then she said, 'My own grandparents were divorced, and my mother grew up fine.' Finally, she said, 'Be sure you tell that to Fanny.' "

"Grandma's grandparents were divorced?" Fanny is astonished. "How come no one ever told me? I didn't think they even had divorce back then."

"Of course they had it," Muffin says. "They just didn't talk so much about it. I didn't even know until last night about my own great-grandparents. But see, I'm telling you now." She and Fanny have both finished eating.

"So," Fanny says, getting up from the table. "Now that Grandma knows, does that mean it isn't a secret anymore?"

"Secret?" says Muffin. "Whoever said it was a secret? We only said it wasn't everybody's business."

"Anybody's." Fanny corrects her. "You said it wasn't anybody's business. In all this time, I never told one person. It's ruined my social life, believe me."

"Well, now you can tell whomever you please," Muffin says

calmly. "I think you'll find, though, people aren't that interested in your personal affairs. They have their own private lives to consider."

Fanny looks doubtful, but doesn't contradict. So much conversation has made her late, again, leaving for school. She grabs her books, kisses her mother, and heads for the door. "Goodbye," she calls back. It will be lunchtime now before she sees Bertha, much less has a chance to tell all her news.

A Dance Recital

Standing in the school yard after lunch, Fanny says to Bertha, "I have something to tell you."

"Yes?" says Bertha.

"My parents are divorced; and my great-great-grandparents were also. It was a long time ago, but I just found it out. Well, I've known about my parents for some time, but not about the other. Even my mother didn't know until last night. It wasn't something people talked about back then." Fanny stops to catch her breath. Bertha doesn't know what to say. She looks somewhat put out. The triplets look interested. Their ears perk up as Fanny rushes on to tell about the boat, as much as she knows.

"I thought we were best friends," Bertha says when Fanny stops talking. Her feelings are hurt. You can tell from her face, and also her voice. "I told you all along about my father," she says. "You knew everything about my family."

Fanny, who has already given this some thought, can understand how Bertha feels. Bertha is her best friend. Fanny would do almost anything not to hurt her. She's come prepared. "I wanted to tell you before now," she says. "But I wasn't supposed to. You remember Mary with her yellow ribbon, don't you? See, it was the same with me as with that girl." Fanny's positive she's told Bertha about Mary before. If so, Bertha doesn't remember.

"I beg your pardon?" she says. "What girl?" She has no idea what Fanny's talking about. Neither have the triplets, but they're curious. That's when Fanny tells them about the girl in the story she knows about from summer camp.

"There was once a girl named Mary who lived next door to a boy named John. They loved each other, and played together every day. Every day, Mary wore a yellow ribbon around her neck. 'Why do you wear that yellow ribbon?' John sometimes asked her. 'I'm not supposed to tell,' she always answered. And she never did. The two of them grew older. They went to school. Every day John carried Mary's books for her, and every day she wore that yellow ribbon. They still loved each other. Now and then John asked her, 'Mary, why do you wear that yellow ribbon around your neck?' But Mary only said, 'Maybe one day I'll tell you, but not yet.' More years passed. They were in junior high, then high school. They were going steady. John loved Mary so, and she loved John. On graduation day, he said, 'Please, won't you tell me now about your yellow ribbon.' 'Not on graduation day,' she said. So that day passed. John and Mary became engaged to be married. They were so in love. 'Mary, honey,' John said, when he gave her the ring, 'now that we're engaged, you'll tell me, won't you, about the yellow ribbon?' 'Maybe on our wedding day,' said Mary. 'Maybe then I'll tell you.' But when their wedding day came, with all the preparations going on, and so much excitement, John forgot to ask. A few days later he remembered. 'Mary, dear,' he said. 'Why do you wear that yellow ribbon all the time?' And Mary said, 'Oh, John. We're married now. We love each other, and we're happy. What difference does it make?' So John let it pass. But he still did want to know. The years went by. They had children. Their children had children. Almost before they knew it, it was John's and Mary's golden wedding anniversary. 'Mary,' John said that morning. 'We've been married fifty years. Please tell me why you wear that yellow ribbon.' Mary said, 'Dear John, you've waited such a long time now. Surely, you can wait a little more. One day, soon, I'll tell you.' More time passed. They were very old, and still they loved each other so. Then, Mary caught a cold that turned into pneumonia. As she lay dying in her bed, John knelt beside her, and he held her hand. 'Dear Mary,' he said. 'I love you so. Please, please won't you tell me now about your yellow ribbon.' Mary looked at John. She loved him, too. 'I guess it's time you knew,' she said. 'You may untie my yellow ribbon.' So John did. And Mary's head fell off.''

Bertha giggles in spite of herself. The triplets pretend to

gasp. They make choking noises in their throats and gargoyle faces.

"See," Fanny says to Bertha. "They were best friends all those years, but still Mary didn't tell John everything she knew. She wasn't supposed to. It was the same way with me."

"I see," Bertha says, but she remains skeptical.

"Anyway," Fanny says. "I have other news to tell you." The triplets listen closely. If anybody else's head, or nose or ears or feet, falls off this time, they want to know it. But all Fanny tells is about her recital. "You're the only one I've told so far, except for my mom," Fanny tells Bertha. "Plus, you're invited. Your whole family is. I've got extra tickets on account of my solo."

"Thank you," says Bertha. She still feels a bit slighted, but she also feels glad for her friend. Fanny looks so happy. Bertha needs time to reflect and sort out her feelings.

SEVERAL DAYS after the children's lunchtime conversation, they all turn up at the thrift shop. It's nothing that they need. They've just stopped by to say "hi" to Ms. O'Leary and find out how she is. Also, they like to keep their eyes on what's new. A peacock feather boa is new in the window. It's silvery green, with turquoise, blue, and purple eyes. It has sequins sewn on and gold tassels.

"Wow," Fanny says, looking out at it now from inside.

Ms. O'Leary removes it from display and lets Fanny try it

on. Fanny looks in the mirror. "It's very becoming," Ms. O'Leary says, standing behind her and fingering the feathers.

"It looks very nice," says Bertha. Having thought things over, she's adopted a forgiving attitude toward Fanny.

"Very glittery," Marc says.

"You look like a movie star," Marvin tells her, reaching out to touch a sequin.

Matthew could not agree more. He thinks Fanny looks beautiful. He's not so sure about the peacock boa though. He eyes its iridescent feathers uneasily. "Don't they look as if they're looking at you?" he asks anyone.

Fanny hardly even hears their compliments, she's so in love with the boa. She discusses price with Ms. O'Leary, and tells her about the recital. "I'm dancing the buggy ride solo," she says. "I think this might be just what I need to complete my costume."

"I'm sure that it is," Ms. O'Leary tells Fanny, and means it.

"I've got my money left I was saving for taps," Fanny explains. "But I want to talk it over first with my mom."

"Of course you do," says Ms. O'Leary. "You just take your time. Don't worry. I'll hold it in back until you make up your mind. It's not the sort of item I get much call for, anyway."

"Thank you," says Fanny.

"Good-bye," the children all say to Ms. O'Leary.

"Good-bye," she says. "Come again soon." She waves as they troop out of her store.

"Those children are just too adorable," Ms. O'Leary tells her husband that evening. She means all five of them. She tells him about Fanny's recital. Then she says, "That Fanny looks so glamorous now she's started thinning down, and Bertha's filled out some, and the triplets have grown at least two inches each since Christmas." Ms. O'Leary could not be more pleased for the sake of the children. Mr. O'Leary could not be more pleased for the sake of his wife. He's a plumber himself, but he sees how running a store can also be rewarding. "It's a good life," he tells Ms. O'Leary, "when you've got the right customers."

By the time Fanny's recital arrives, she's more than prepared. She's got all her steps down perfectly, and she certainly does look glamorous. She has on a custom-made cowgirl costume, with white patent tap boots, fringes, and chaps. Draped dramatically across both her shoulders, with one tasseled end flung back over her neck, is the green and turquoise, blue and purple, sequined peacock feather boa she purchased from Ms. O'Leary.

"Doesn't Fanny look beautiful?" her grandparents say to each other. They're seated side by side in the front row, next to Muffin and Hildegarde. Bertha is sitting with both her parents and the triplets, somewhere mid-orchestra. Fanny's father has an aisle seat toward the back of the auditorium. Sitting beside him is a willowy blonde in a tight-fitting dress nearly covered in rhinestones whom he'd introduced earlier to Fanny.

"Fanny, meet Honey Lefkowitz," he said. "She's an up-and-coming country-singer star. Honey, this is Fanny."

"I'm pleased to meet you," Fanny told her, politely.

"Likewise, I'm sure," Honey said.

"She's some new client from Nashville he runs around with," Fanny's mother tells her own mother, who is this minute sitting turned around in her seat, peering at Honey through a pair of opera glasses.

"She's awfully thin, isn't she?" Fanny's grandmother says, but just then the music starts, and everyone gets quiet. The curtain rises, and there is Fanny, standing center-stage, lit up by multicolored floodlights. One of her knees is slightly bent,

and her toes are turned out correctly. Some oohs and aahs are heard from the audience as she begins her routine and executes, with apparent ease, even the most difficult parts. Her timing and posture are perfect.

Afterward, when the program is over and Fanny takes her bows, everyone claps very loudly. "Bravo," shouts Fanny's grandfather from his seat. Then so do a few of the others. Someone approaches the stage and hands Fanny two bouquets of long-stemmed roses. She curtseys gracefully as she takes them. Backstage, she reads the cards.

"From Mom. I'm proud of you, and I love you very much," says one.

"Congratulations. Love, Bernie and Honey," reads the other.

Later, Fanny gets a third card, handmade by Bertha. A

picture of a cowgirl climbing down from a buggy is pasted on front. Printed inside is a verse: "We think you're grand, we think you're svelte, we're glad to see you dance so well." It's been signed by all of the Segals.

Fanny's picture is in the local paper the next day, *The Tenafly Times*, alongside a brief review of the recital. "Fanny Barton danced with aplomb," reads the caption.

"It's a great shot," Bertha tells Fanny. "You look beautiful."

"Thank you," says Fanny. "But I think it's mostly the way the boa is draped that makes me look thinner."

Fanny's mother thinks Fanny looks beautiful, too. She cuts the picture out, frames it, and keeps it on her desk. "You look like a star," she tells Fanny. "I'm sure you'll go far. You only need the right agent."

Everybody
Sometime After

"BYE, FANNY! Bye, Bertha!" The other children call out to the two best friends as they walk home from school. The girls are in the sixth grade now. Autumn's in the air, and there's a breeziness in both girls' strides. Their lives have seldom seemed so pleasant. Any family problems they encounter are only ordinary, and name-calling is just a memory. In fact, they've become quite popular in school. Publicity has given them an edge. In Fanny's case it came from dancing, and in Bertha's case from sponges, as we're about to see.

The triplets are also doing fine. Of course, they never lacked publicity. Just turning up was always sufficient. Even so, they seem more lighthearted since their father's come back. It makes them feel safer just having him home, and they love to help him in his store, Segals' Sponge and Seashell Market. He sells everything that pertains to marine life, including books.

"I know the business now," he said when he first started. "Plus, I've got the right connections." He meant Mr. Ortiz, his wholesale supplier. Money wasn't a problem. Mr. Segal had put some aside sponging in Florida, with no family there to spend it on. He also received back pay for all the time he'd been away from his regular job. He hadn't been unemployed, after all, only missing in the line of duty.

"Military hardware's a good living," he said when he quit, "but a family man doesn't want to travel so much. Besides, I like sponges. Tenafly seems a good place for my store." He ticked off the good points on his fingers: "It's not far from water, no competition, and you don't see too many alligators in New Jersey."

"Any," Bertha said, when she repeated all of this to Fanny. Actually, Bertha likes sponges, too. By this time, the whole family does. Bertha also likes helping in the store. After school and on weekends, she and her brothers dust, stock shelves, make change at the cash register, and sometimes roll pennies to trade at the bank. When business is slow, they read books on the seashore.

Their mother helps when she has time, but usually she's too busy. She gave up both her jobs and went back to college to become a librarian. "It's a good job for a person like me who likes reading," she said when she started. "So many books, after all." She also thought this, but didn't say it: What happened once *could* happen twice. She knows it isn't likely, but just in case her husband ever does get lost again and have amnesia, she'll be prepared. She won't be standing on her feet all day, holding down two jobs. Next time, she'll have a profession.

" 'Librarian' is certainly more practical than 'farmer' when you live in Tenafly," Bertha told Fanny the day her mother registered for classes. It was that same day when the Segals' picture, taken in front of the store, was published in *The Tenafly Times*. "Family of the Year" read the caption underneath it. An article described how Simon Segal was lost, then found, and how his family carried on bravely while he was gone.

"I don't know how we would have managed without Bertha's help," Ms. Segal told the reporter.

The article also brought readers up-to-date on the family's current affairs, including Ms. Segal in school.

Mr. Segal clipped both article and picture, and put them in his store window for customers to see. Hallie at her Hotcake House and Caesar in his Pizza Palace did the same. They admire the Segals; so do the customers. "That's some family," they say. "Aren't those children adorable!" They mean all four of them. This is how they look in the picture: The triplets are standing in front, a bit short, perhaps, for fourth grade, but just about right for their age. Matthew is on the left. He still looks a smidgen taller than his brothers. He has his spiral notebook tucked under one arm and is holding onto a cap with one hand. Marc is the one in the middle wearing the bow tie. Marvin is on the right, waving. They are all three standing very straight, trying to look taller. Bertha is standing behind them, one parent on either side. Her hair is brushed back from her forehead. Not a single frown line is showing. She has definitely put on some weight, though she's still on the slim side. No doubt, being thin's in her nature. She's smiling, though, and you can see how her face has filled out. How pretty she looks in the picture. All the Segals are smiling.

"It's a good-looking family, isn't it?" the customers say to one another.

Fanny brought home a copy of the paper the day the story appeared. "What a good idea," Hildegarde said when she read it. She meant the part about Ms. Segal going back to college. Hildegarde thought it through carefully. The next day she showed up on campus herself and registered for night classes. She's earning a degree now in automotive mechanics. "A person who knows how to do something with her hands can always get a job," she told Fanny. "I'm good with mine, plus I already know a thing or two about engines from growing up on a ranch; vans, tractors, jeeps, or trailers, something was always breaking down."

Hildegarde also bought a saxophone. She plans to teach herself to play it. "I want to get so I can make it talk," she told Fanny. "Who knows? After I retire, I may join a band, or have my own radio show, or go on TV. Or, I might just follow in my aunt Emma's footsteps, and become a water witch, putting on concerts for wildlife. See, you're growing up," she said. "You won't need me forever."

Fanny would have liked to protest. She loves Hildegarde, and cannot imagine life without her. Ever since Fanny can remember, Hildegarde's been there. But she knew what Hildegarde said was true. Fanny needs her less already. Muffin's home more often now for one thing. She installed an office in the house last summer, in what once was Bernie's den. She added a second phone line, put in a fax machine and a computer. She divided up the business.

"I'm keeping the East Coast clients," she told Bernie, the

day he moved out. "You can take the rest." She informed Hildegarde next. "From now on, I'll be working from home," she said. "Fanny's father and I are divorced. He's moving on." Hildegarde didn't seem surprised. The last thing Muffin did that day was telephone her mother. "Fanny's not a baby anymore," she said. "I think as girls get older, they need their mothers more. Besides, I never did like traveling. Whenever I was gone, I always missed Fanny."

Fanny herself is doing fine, and of course she's still dancing. She likes having her mother at home, though sometimes she misses her father. "Mom" and "Dad" she calls them now. Muffin no longer corrects her.

"Mom's got a nice ring," she said to her own mom.

"I always thought it did," Fanny's grandmother replied.

Fanny's mom did turn out right about this: When Fanny tells other children about her parents' divorce, they aren't that interested. Only the part about the houseboat is apt to capture their attention.

Fanny spent quite a few weekends on it during the summer. She turned out to be an excellent sailor. So did Bertha and the triplets. Last weekend, they all were aboard. Honey was also there. Fanny's father was right about this: his boat has plenty of room.

The boys played a game of shuffleboard on deck before dinner. Bernie stood with his back to the railing and watched them.

"I bet, if those boys learned a few tricks, they could clean up in show business," he said to anyone.

"Really," said Fanny. She did a little shuffle hop step on deck to keep warm, and pulled her boa around her shoulders more tightly, fluffing its feathers. She's certainly gotten her money's worth.

"Sure," said her father. "I saw boy triplets last month cleaning up in Las Vegas. It was a tumbling act with a father who tapped."

Bertha interrupted. "They've already got jobs," she said. "Our family's in sponges. Besides, they're not allowed to travel. They're too young." The triplets were relieved hearing this. They could not agree more.

Later, at home, Fanny recounted the conversation to her mother and Hildegarde.

"Really?" her mother said. "Isn't that amazing!" She meant, of course, the part about the triplets in Las Vegas.

"I'm not surprised," said Hildegarde. She meant about anything.